Dear Parents:

Congratulations! Your child is taking the first steps on an exciting journey. The destination? Independent reading!

STEP INTO READING® will help your child get there. The program offers five steps to reading success. Each step includes fun stories and colorful art or photographs. In addition to original fiction and books with favorite characters, there are Step into Reading Non-Fiction Readers, Phonics Readers and Boxed Sets, Sticker Readers, and Comic Readers—a complete literacy program with something to interest every child.

Learning to Read, Step by Step!

Ready to Read   Preschool–Kindergarten
• big type and easy words • rhyme and rhythm • picture clues
For children who know the alphabet and are eager to begin reading.

Reading with Help   Preschool–Grade 1
• basic vocabulary • short sentences • simple stories
For children who recognize familiar words and sound out new words with help.

Reading on Your Own   Grades 1–3
• engaging characters • easy-to-follow plots • popular topics
For children who are ready to read on their own.

Reading Paragraphs   Grades 2–3
• challenging vocabulary • short paragraphs • exciting stories
For newly independent readers who read simple sentences with confidence.

Ready for Chapters   Grades 2–4
• chapters • longer paragraphs • full-color art
For children who want to take the plunge into chapter books but still like colorful pictures.

STEP INTO READING® is designed to give every child a successful reading experience. The grade levels are only guides; children will progress through the steps at their own speed, developing confidence in their reading. The F&P Text Level on the back cover serves as another tool to help you choose the right book for your child.

Remember, a lifetime love of reading starts with a single step!

To my three boys, who grow like weeds.
I will always love you through every season!
—D.D.

To young readers everywhere
—A.K.

All rights reserved. Published in the United States by Random House Children's Books, a division of Penguin Random House LLC, New York.

Step into Reading, Random House, and the Random House colophon are registered trademarks of Penguin Random House LLC.

Visit us on the Web!
rhcbooks.com

Educators and librarians, for a variety of teaching tools, visit us at RHTeachersLibrarians.com

Library of Congress Cataloging-in-Publication Data is available upon request.
ISBN 978-0-593-18049-5 (trade) — ISBN 978-0-593-18051-8 (lib. bdg.) —
ISBN 978-0-593-18050-1 (ebook)

Printed in the United States of America
10 9 8 7 6 5 4 3 2 1
First Edition

This book has been officially leveled by using the F&P Text Level Gradient™ Leveling System.

Misty the Cloud
The Thing About Spring

by Dylan Dreyer
with Alan Katz
illustrated by Rosie Butcher

Random House 🏠 New York

Clare and her mom
were doing some
spring cleaning.

They made piles of
books and clothes
to give away.

baby
books

As Clare
packed up boxes,
she asked her mother
why they always
cleaned for spring.

Clare's mom told her
that spring is
a season of change.

"In late March,
the top half
of the earth
tilts closer to the sun.
Nights will get shorter.

"Days will get longer . . . and warmer.

And flowers will bloom once again."

That gave Clare
an idea.
She found her flower kit.

It was the perfect time
for Clare to
plant her seeds!

Misty and her mom
were also doing some
spring cleaning.
"Done!" said Misty.

"Spring cleaning
is not just about
making your room
look nice,"
her mom said.

Grass
Trees
flowers
lakes
streams
fields

“In spring,
clouds also
need to rain
to fill the lakes
and streams.

"We must water
the trees,

the flowers,

and the grass."

Our rain helps green things grow tall and strong!

Back at Clare's house,
Clare planted
her seeds in the soil.
She gave them
a tiny bit of water.
She placed the pot
on the back deck.

"Now what?" Clare asked.

"Now we wait,"
her mother said.

"Raining is fun!"
Misty cheered.
"It's a blast!"
Wispy added.

Nimby asked them why
nothing was growing.

Raye the sunbeam
and her friends
showed up.
Raye told Nimby
they needed to help
make things grow, too.

"Our sunshine
warms the earth.
The sun helps
plants to grow," she said.

Raye and Misty
made up a little song.

*You give rain
and I give sun!*

Teaming up for
plants is fun!

Clare looked in her
flowerpot every day.
One day, she saw
a tiny green shoot.
"It is starting
to grow, Mom!"
shouted Clare.

After one month,
the plant
was standing tall.

After two months,
the flower was
ready to bloom.

Clare's flower
had bloomed.
It was a great big
sunflower!

She handed it to
her mom.
"This is for you!"

"Great job, everyone!" said Misty's mom. She looked so proud.

"How pretty the earth
gets in spring!"
she said.

Hooray for spring!